CREATED BY BERNICE CHARDIET

THE ROUGH, GRUFF GOAT BROTHERS RAP

WRITTEN BY JON CHARDIET
ILLUSTRATED BY J. C. SUARES

SCHOLASTIC INC.
New York   Toronto   London   Auckland   Sydney

HERE WE GO!
HERE WE GO!

ISBN 0-590-45860-4

Copyright © 1993 by Chardiet Unlimited, Inc.
Illustrations © 1993 by J.C. Suares.
All rights reserved. Published by Scholastic Inc.
CARTWHEEL BOOKS is a trademark of Scholastic Inc.
RAP TALES is a trademark of Chardiet Unlimited, Inc.

12 11 10 9 8 7 6 5 4 3 2 1   3 4 5 6 7/9

Printed in the U.S.A.   09

First Scholastic printing, March 1993

Way up in the mountains, all covered with snow,
was a place where people didn't like to go.
It was dangerous and scary, but that wasn't the reason
that everyone avoided it in every season.

Nobody liked the rickety bridge
that crossed the mountains at the highest ridge.

You see, people were scared to pay the toll
because the bridge, for a keeper, had a nasty old troll.

Now, all trolls are nasty, but this one was the worst.
In a line of ugly trolls, he'd be the first.
He had a big green head and a large hairy nose.
He had so much hair, he didn't need any clothes.

His mouth was as big as a garbage can.
He could swallow a cow or swallow a man.
He had big, big hands and bigger feet,
and when people crossed the bridge, he yelled,

"Gimme my meat!"

One day the ugly troll was taking a nap,
when upon the bridge he heard a *trip, tip, tap.*
He poked his head up and said, "Who could that be?"
Said a tiny little voice, "It's only me.

"It's me, the first billy goat gruff.
When I grow up, I'll be rough and tough.
I've got two brothers who are really buff.
Their fleece is fluff, but they've got the right stuff."

The troll saw a billy goat with skinny little legs.
Said the troll, "I think I'll eat you up like scrambled eggs."
Said the goat, "Don't take me! You won't get enough.
Just wait for my brothers, the billy goats gruff."

The troll thought a minute and said, "OK.
You're too small for breakfast anyway.

"I'll wait for your brother, and then I'll dine.
I'll use his brain for baking and his blood for wine."

The troll went back to continue his nap.
But on the bridge he heard a *trip, tip, tap.*
He poked his head up and saw standing there
a much larger billy goat with a strong, steady stare.

"It's me, my man, the second billy goat gruff.
No piece of fluff and getting tough.
Someday, like my brother, I'll be so buff.
But right now I'm just tough enough."

Said the troll, "You're bigger! It'll be a delight
to gobble you up and feed my appetite."
Said the goat, "Let me give you a tip.
You'll wait and eat my brother if you're really hip."

The troll thought a minute and said, "OK.
A big meal's better than two small ones anyway."
He let the second goat cross with a *trip, tip, tap.*
And he sat back down to continue his nap.

But then he heard a very loud sound.
The bridge swayed so much, it almost fell to the ground.
He yelled, "Who's that tramping while I'm trying to sleep?"
Then he heard a voice that was loud and deep.

"It's me, it's me, the third billy goat gruff!
As you can see, I'm rough and tough.
I'm buff. I've got the stuff.
I'm tougher than the toughest,
and that's tough enough."

The third billy goat was big and strong.
His legs were big, and his horns were long.
He wiggled his tail and shook his head,
and in a deep voice, this is what he said.

"I'm gonna get you, troll, with my two spears.
I'm gonna poke your eyeballs out of your ears.
My horns are long and strong as stone.
I'm gonna crush you to bits, body and bone!"

They battled till the bridge began to swing and sway.
And the goat rammed the troll and blew him away,
squashed the troll's head and kicked his hairy hide,
and tossed the troll, screaming, over the side.

Then the billy goats gruff went on their way
to the meadow where there was so much hay
that they never crossed back over the ridge
where the troll used to guard that rickety bridge.